MORi's FAMILY ADVENTURES

By Geiszel Godoy

Copyright © 2018 Geiszel Godoy

Illustrations by
David Lenormand

Colors by
David Lenormand & Huan Lim

Creative Director
Manuel Godoy

Publisher
Black Sands Entertainment, Inc.
Queens, New York

ISBN: 978-0-9994734-7-4

Dedication

This book is dedicated to my wonderful children
Mori and Valencia. Also my niece and nephews
(Riley, Ryan, Matthew, Taylor, Victor Jr., Joseph,
and Zavion). They love to read books and we have
an amazing time taking family trips together.

I would like to thank God for making this all
possible for me. Also the fans who support Black
Sands Entertainment. Especially the Kickstarter and
Patrons backer. Thank you so much for your loyalty
and contributions!

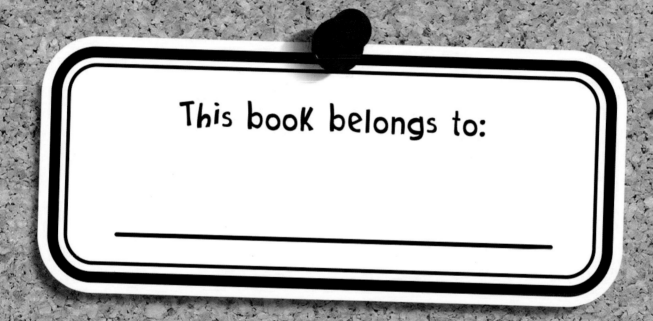

This book belongs to:

_____

Dad came into the room with new suitcases, and we immediately started packing our clothes and shoes for the trip. Valencia and I assisted Mom and Dad with our best efforts.
"We'll have to leave very early in the morning if we do not want to miss our flight, kids," said Dad.

The next day, we got up early and made it to the airport on time. Valencia and I sat beside Grandma on the plane. During our long flight, we talked about the amazing Brazilian places that we knew of, and where we want to go when we arrive at Rio de Janeiro, Brazil.

Our family went to enjoy the Copacabana Beach.
We made a big splash in the ocean.
"This water is so refreshing!" exclaimed Mom.
Dad warned, "Mori and Valencia, look out for the waves!"
"It looks like you guys are having lots of fun!" Grandma
called out to us from the shore.

Our whole family enjoyed spending the entire evening on the
beach together. We watched the sun set from the shore.

When we finally reached the top of the Sugarloaf Mountain, our family was amazed by the mesmerizing landscape!

I called out to my little sister, "We are currently 395 meters above the ground, Valencia!" "There are small islands all around the area, and the large buildings in the city look as small as my toys at home," she replied with a smile.

Just a couple of days later, we found ourselves on a wild jeepney ride to the depths of Tijuca Rainforest! With our hands in the air, my sister and I spotted beautiful animals during the trip.

"Look!" I pointed towards a large bird. "There is a Hyacinth Macaw over there!" "Did you know that the Hyacinth Macaw is the largest of all Macaw species?" our tour guide stated. "Although they are the largest parrot species, they are sweet and known as "gentle giants".
"Just like Dad!" Valencia exclaimed, making Mom giggle.

"Mori, look at those monkeys swinging on trees!" Valencia pointed out.
"I would love to swing on those trees too!" I replied, imagining how great
it would be to join them.
"You have to grow tall and strong to swing on trees, Mori,"
added Grandma who stood right behind us.

We reached the Taunay Waterfall Area and Picnic Area, where our family was able to witness such a breathtaking waterfall. We were also able to see some sloths and squirrels, and take pictures of the Coati, a type of raccoon known for its pointy nose and ringed tail.
"This is truly the best trip ever!"

A couple of days later, Mom and Dad got us some tickets to see the Samba Parade. We arrived at the Sambadrome just an hour before the show started, and it was huge!
"Today, we are going to witness samba performances by thousands of dancers," said Dad.

"Dad," I pointed out to some familiar faces. "Is that the Gore family?"
"You are right, Mori!" exclaimed Mom happily.
"There's Susan and Paul, along with the kids!"
"Mori, let's go say hi to Chanequa, Carlton and Teon!" said Valencia.

We approached our friends and decided to watch the Samba Parade together. Soon enough, a loud bang was heard and music filled the dome as the dancers emerged. They wore colorful costumes, and some of them looked like they were wearing wings on their backs! All of them danced samba beautifully and the crowd cheered for them. It was a beautiful sight to behold!

After such a wonderful week in Rio de Janeiro, our vacation trip is coming to an end. Mom decided to buy souvenirs for all of our friends at home, but we were unexpectedly greeted by a monkey friend! "Wait!" cried Valencia. "Please give my teddy bear back!"

Until we reached the outside of Candelária Church and found the owner of the monkey. It was a Brazilian kid, who smiled as bright as the sun upon receiving the teddy bear.

We approached him, and my sister decided to give the teddy bear to the friendly Brazilian kid, to make him even happier. "Let's take a picture together!" said Dad while holding onto the camera. While our trip came to an end, we'll never forget the experiences and memories we made together on this journey!

Copacabana Beach
in Rio

The Escadaria Selarón
is the world famous steps in
Rio de Janeiro, Brazil

Rio de Janeiro,
Brazil

Christ the Redeemer,
New 7 Wonders Of The World

Tijuca Forest is the world largest urban tropical rainforest

The Chinese view inside of the Tijuca forest

About the author:

Geiszel Godoy is an Army Veteran, wife, and mother of two beautiful children who loves to travel the world together. She studied Fashion Design in California at the Art Institute of San Diego. Also Fashion Business Management at FIT in NYC. She worked in the Fashion Capital of NYC as a Technical Designer. Geiszel and her husband love to travel with their kids to experience fun and kid friendly adventures. This is what inspired her to write her children's book Mori's Family Adventures.

Geiszel is also the Author of :
Mori's Family Adventures South Africa,
Brazilian Culture Exchange,
Mori's Family Adventures World Traveling Coloring Book Vol # 1

THANK YOU

Kickstarter Backers

Calvin L Jones

Morris Green

Adiyia Duncan

Barrington

Ricardo Thomas

Tiffany Hurt

Fredrick West

Lynette Abott

Allen Murray

Mr James A Tate

Ethan Agbandje

Dana Morgan

Rizzy Toole

Amisi Kalonda

Aaron Jameson

Bim Akinkuowo

Paul Agard

jason lee sneed

Leslie Cribbs

Thomas Brinkley

Christopher Mookie Walker

Darnell Coleman

Jervay Wright

Curtis Ewing

Susan Gore

Jennifer Taylor

Derrick Ward

Cleo Dishmon

Pertrell Mallett

Stan Livingston

Steve Ramos

Joy Cato

Mori's Family Adventures

By Geiszel Godoy

Illustrations by
David Lenormand

Creative Director
Manuel Godoy

Instagram: Instagram.com/Mori__Adventures

Facebook: https://www.Facebook.com/MoriAdventures

Email: geiszel@blacksandsentertainment.com

Store page: BuyKids2Kings.com